SHE-MALE SEDUCTIONS 2 "Surprise Package"
She-Male Erotica

by
Blake Worthington

CHANCES PRESS
www.chancespress.com

She-Male Seductions 2: Surprise Package
Copyright 2008 by Blake Worthington

Published by Chances Press, Las Vegas, NV

Cover Design by Geronimo Quitoriano
www.gpolaroid.com

Queen Sized

I had just bought into one those new loft developments on Hollywood Boulevard. You know the ones: gutted historic buildings now with the rooftop pool, exposed brick walls, concrete floors, high ceilings, granite countertops, stainless steel appliances and the requisite young urbanites revitalizing the neglected inner city.

I remember when the building was a department store, shopping as a young kid with my mother. The area was a bit rundown then and getting rougher as more affluent families fled to the malls and suburbs. Out went the glamorous Hollywood and in came the wig shops, adult bookstores and prostitutes: the things that made Hollywood **HOLLYWOOD** to a young kid. But now the area was becoming hip again, and I figured I better buy now before I get priced out of the old neighborhood.

Not bad for a transgender just shy of her thirtieth birthday. I worked hard not getting killed at Hollywood High School and after a few years finished law school. I work for a small firm of dedicated lawyers who help out small nonprofits in the city (very rewarding albeit low paying). But I still managed to pay off student loans and save up for a down payment on the loft condo.

I just got the keys yesterday

and so was running around padding the nest. Not too much, mind you. I'm not one of those fancy label types who has to buy or wear the latest and greatest. I consider myself a pretty simple gal, and I like it like that. And besides, I already blew most of my money on the down payment, so less is VERY more for me right now. My last purchase of the day was also one of the most expensive--a bed. The last few years I'd been slumming it on the futon that saw me through college and law school. Though I've had my share of kinky guys into t-girls on that futon (fellow classmates, closeted jocks, starving actors and even an extremely kinky visiting Associate Professor from Ireland), my sometimes aching back was telling me it was time for an upgrade. A queen size would fit perfectly in the new place.

I had passed by the store, "Bedopolis," too many times to count on my way into the office. Their huge sign had their slogan underneath: "Your Bed Is Our Business. Family Owned and Operated since 1954." I imagined the owner to be some crotchety old man complaining about the big box stores with their cheap imports and cattle-call customer service.

I parked my car in front of the store. It was late Friday night almost 8:30pm. I had a day off and was saving the biggest purchase for the end of the day. There was only one other car in the lot whose license plate read "BED MAN." Must be old crotchety's car, I thought to myself. I walked in and a sensor triggered a little "ding dong" bell sound in the showroom like in those Korean owned liquor stores. For a small business, they had some nice stuff inside. I looked around. Clean, modern looking beds lined the store. Classical music pumped through the sound system. Good presentation, nice overhead lighting and a fresh palette of bed coverings suggested a designer's eye. I was impressed.

"How can I help you?" a voice asked from behind me. I was too busy imagining one of the beds in my new place to hear footsteps.

I turned around and found

myself in the company of a fresh faced young man in his early 20's with a nice build and strong square jaw wearing a crisp shirt and silk tie. He had short cropped dark hair and piercing brown eyes. He had the exotic look reminiscent of an old silent screen star.

I needed a second to compose myself. This was a pleasant surprise. Very pleasant. "Yes, I'm looking for a new bed— a queen sized," I explained.

The young man introduced himself as Nate. He told me his father owned the business but that he'd take over weekend evenings for the old man. Nate was finishing up his design major at a local art school. *A man after my own heart*, I thought. Besides myself, he seemed to be the only one left in the store.

Nate went skillfully into his spiel: "We spend a third of our lives in bed, so a high quality bed with good support is essential."

"How long does a mattress usually last?" I asked, keeping the matter very professional even though I wanted to rip his clothes off, lift my skirt up and fuck his brains out on the platform bed in the corner.

"Well it depends on how much use it gets. Whether it's supporting one or two bodies and factors like pregnancy or weight gain," Nathan explained matter-of-factly.

"Well, in that case, since I'm

single and don't plan on getting pregnant anytime soon, mine should last forever," I joked. It wasn't far from the truth. I've had so many legal cases lately my social life was like my old futon: kinda sad looking and in desperate need of a makeover. I haven't had a gentleman caller in a while.

"Really? I'm surprised a beautiful woman like you is single," Nate remarked emphatically. "We'll have to take care of that," he added.

Was he flirting with me? I wondered.

"Here, lie on this." He pointed to a mattress nearby. "This memory foam molds to your body. Lie on your back and take off your shoes. Relax..." he coaxed.

I didn't mind taking orders from the delectable dreamboat in front of me. I took off my sensible pumps and lay on the bed that was strewn with throw pillows. The pressures of the hectic day started to melt away.

"Aahhh, that feels nice," I purred.

"You can test a bed's firmness by placing your hand under the small of your back while lying flat. If there's a gap, it's too hard. If you can't get a hand underneath, it's too soft. Can I show you...?" he asked.

"Oh, please do." I was as relaxed as a wet noodle and just wanted to lay there with Nate. He placed his hand under my back. I guess I knew what Goldilocks felt: Not too hard, not too soft, but just right.

"How's that feel?" Nate asked. His warm, soft hand had slipped under my skirt and was rubbing my lower back, some of his fingers brushing inside the waistband of my panties. If this is part of his sales technique, I was offering no resistance.

"Well, you could go a little lower," I teased.

"No problem. As my dad says, 'The customer is always right.'"

His hand under my back delved down my shorts, and Nate began to knead my butt muscles. His other hand was massaging my inner thigh, brushing close to my balls.

"Ah, I see you've got a little

something extra down here. I really like that..." Nate said.

By this time I had a raging hard-on as stiff as a bedpost. He pulled off my skirt and yanked my black panties to my ankles.

He climbed onto the bed and straddled my knees. He grabbed my she-dick in one hand while the other was massaging one of my breasts. He teased my dick head with his tongue, licking off the drop of precum forming at my piss slit. He licked my balls and placed tender kisses around my whole crotch area. For a young guy, he was very patient and skilled. I grabbed one of the satin throw pillows and placed it over my mouth to muffle my cries of pleasure.

After almost taking me to the edge, he sweetly asked, "So, do you want to fuck me?"

"Yes, as soon as I saw you. I want to fuck you so bad, Nate," was my quick reply. It was true. This young stud was turning me on. So help me God. Though I loved getting fucked, I'm fully functional and am not shy about it.

He led me into a large storeroom in the back. It was wall to wall mattresses--all still wrapped in plastic, ready for delivery. He took off his shirt and tie, kicked off his shoes and dropped his pants. I could see his erection through his cotton boxers. He was pretty smooth and had only a little hair on his chest, arms and legs. I pulled his boxers down and hungrily went down on his thick manmeat. I wanted to show him the same attention he was giving me in the showroom. He gently grabbed my head and pulled my long hair away from my face as I made love to him with my mouth, lips and tongue.

"Oh, girl, that feels so good," Nate moaned.

I could tell he was getting close, but I wanted him to cum while I was inside him. I turned him around and had him lay face down on a nearby mattress. I had him stick his ass up so I could pay homage to its perfect roundness. It was just as smooth as the rest of him. I spread his butt cheeks wide and licked his quivering hole. He begged, "Please, please fuck me now."

I stood up and grabbed a condom from one of the pockets in my purse and placed it on my rock hard dick. I had Nate get up on his hands and knees, with his ass up in the air at the edge of the bed. I stood up and aimed my dick at his eagerly awaiting hole.

I plunged in, and he let out a small cry. He was really tight. I myself had to inhale sharply as my dick went into his hot, tight ass. I let my dick sit in him for a second, letting his ass get used to having a hot transexual's dick inside. I then started pumping slowly, not wanting the pleasure to end. I varied the rhythm and almost would pull out only to plunge even deeper. I could feel my dick each time it pressed against his prostate and Nate would grunt out, "Yeah, girl. Fuck me. That t-dick feels so good up my ass!"

I bent down over him and he turned his head so our lips could touch. I had one hand supporting his chest while I fucked the shit out of him. My other hand reached around to his dick. I was pumping his tool with each thrust of mine into his tight ass.

"Oh, fuck, I'm going to come," he moaned. I jacked him off even faster, and I could feel his dick expand as he bent his head and neck back sharply. He shot a huge load onto the plastic sheeting over the mattress and gobs of it covered my hand. The touch and sight of the young stud's hot jizm sent me over the edge. I grabbed his hips and made a few more deep thrusts into his hole. I let out a loud cry as my whole body felt it was being shot out of my dick. It was the most amazing orgasm I've ever had.

I pulled out of Nate and we collapsed on top of the bed. We were both sweaty and breathing heavily. I kissed him tenderly.

"Girl, that was really hot," he said with a satisfied smile.

"Yeah, I feel the same way. Um, I hope this doesn't sound out of place, but I just wanted to let you know I would've taken the bed even if we hadn't…you know," I said, my voice trailing off. I wasn't sure if I should say anything or if I was making things more awkward.

"No worries. I would've…you know...even if we hadn't...even if I didn't close the deal," he said sincerely.

We dressed up, and afterwards he had me fill out all the required paperwork. He led me to the front door, shook my hand quite professionally. I couldn't believe such a fantastic evening was over so soon.

"Oh, by the way," Nate said as I walked to my car, "on Saturdays my dad schedules me as the delivery guy. So, I'll bring over the bed tomorrow and assemble it for you. It's all part of the service, you know, to make sure the customer is happy."

Let's just say that my back is now ache free. And lately, Nate and I have been seriously putting a dent in the ten year life span of my wonderful new bed. At this rate, I may have to buy a new mattress every year! And when I do, you can bet it's gonna be from Bedopolis.

Rose Bud

I stared out the window as the sun slowly set behind the Hollywood Hills. Outside my office door, I could hear the chatter of my officemates talking about their plans and wishing others a good weekend. I'd spent the whole day cooped up in my office at the advertising firm I worked for trying to come up with a jingle for a new smoothie chain. We'll actually that's a lie. I was really thinking about *him*. He'd been all I could think of for the past week. How much I missed him, how much I wanted to touch him, and have him penetrate me haunted my every thought.

"Kylie, are you still working?" my co-worker Megan said,

popping her curly haired head through my office door. "It is Friday you know."

"I just want to wrap up some work on this Smoothie Smooth account," I answered feebly.

Megan walked into my office, dropped her Prada bag on my desk and sat down.

"Girl, you've been holed up in this office for days," she said. "And I know it doesn't have a damn thing to do with Smoothie Smooth. You're thinking about *him*. You're obsessing, you know?"

"That obvious, huh?" I said, pushing my chair back from my desk and kicking off my Gucci pumps.

Megan and I were more than co-workers, we'd become pretty

good friends over the past few years. She didn't flinch when I confessed to her I was a transwoman. We often lunched together along Little Santa Monica Boulevard in Beverly Hills during the week and spilled our guts about the man troubles in our lives. "You're going to give in, aren't you? Megan said, shaking her head.

"Well, he says he's sorry. That he knows what he wants now."

Megan leaned across my desk and locked eyes with me.

"Kylie, they always say that."

I sighed and said, "I know."

My on again off again boyfriend, Ryan, had announced two

weeks ago over a candlelight dinner at my favorite bistro in Santa Monica that he wasn't sure what he wanted in terms of a relationship and maybe we needed a "break."

Distraught, I had spent days in bed watching old Lana Turner movies and eating fattening specialty ice cream. Then, of course, as if right on cue, Ryan called and said he had made a terrible mistake. That he had just been scared. Wouldn't I give him another chance? *Again?*

I had summoned up all my strength, told him I needed to think about what I wanted, and then I called Megan and whined, "He says he's sorry."

"He's just constantly keeping you off balance," Megan had said.

I could visualize her rolling her eyes on the other end of the phone.

"Come on let's go grab some dinner," Megan said, standing up, obviously ready to begin the weekend.

"Maybe next time," I replied. "I just need a quiet evening. And despite what you said, I really do have to work on the Smoothie Smooth account."

"Fine, but you need to have some fun- *without Ryan*. He's just playing you. Don't fall for it!"

After Megan left, I tried to focus on my computer screen, but it was pointless. I kept looking at the phone, wondering if I should pick it up and call Ryan.

"Uh, hi, miss," a husky male voice said suddenly.

I jumped in my chair. "Excuse me?"

In walked a tall muscular young Latino, he couldn't have been more than twenty, had dimples to die for, and nicely developed biceps--big, but not steroid big, a natural man. In his hand, he held a dozen deep pink roses, my favorites.

"I didn't mean to scare you," he said. "I have a delivery for a Kylie Mills. I got a little lost on the way here. I apologize."

He wiped some sweat from his forehead with his one free hand so I caught a glimpse of his pec muscles ripple.

"I'm Kylie Mills," I said, sounding less than enthusiastic. The roses had Ryan written all over them. He knew I was a sucker for flowers.

"These are for you," the guy said, handing the roses off to me.

"Thanks," I said, taking them and setting them on my desk like an unwanted new stack of work. It angered me that Ryan thought I was that easy to move. Was I? "Hold on a second."

I reached for my purse in my for some cash to get a tip, pulled it out, and then discovered the only cash I had on me was a dollar bill.   I hadn't even made it to the ATM in days.

"I'm so sorry," I said.   "I usually have more cash than this."

"It's okay, miss.   Don't worry about it," he replied.

I could feel his eyes on me, studying my bootylicious body.   As a result, I could feel a rush of heat coarse through me.   Then I told myself I was just reading into the situation.   I was past thirty.   What would this lean defined young guy with dark intense eyes and a full basket below want with me when even Ryan couldn't decide about me after three years?

"Here," I said, my French manicured fingers handing over the little cash I had.

He hesitated, and then he waved a hand.

"Keep it. This one's on me," he said, beaming a bright smile. "I had a hard time finding you in here. I think the rest of your office is gone."

"Yeah, burning the midnight oil," I said.

He looked truly interested in what I had to say. Maybe I was fantasizing, but when was the last time a guy did that?

"I gotta say, most gals...," he began.

Did he just call me a "gal?"

"Are pretty happy to get flowers. Boyfriend, I'm guessing," he said, smiling.

"Ex-boyfriend," I replied.

He nodded knowingly. "Well, his loss. Have a good night."

I watched as he walked out of the office, at his perfectly shaped butt that begged to be tasted, and thought about how many times in my life when I was younger I missed out on being with a hot guy because I was just focused on some ass who couldn't decide if he wanted me.

All of a sudden, I felt decadent, brazen, and wanted to throw caution to the wind. Why did I always sit around waiting for the man to make all of the moves? Hoping that he'd look my way.

"Excuse me!" I called after the delivery guy.

I heard him turn around and his footsteps headed back to my office.

I got up from behind my desk and unbuttoned the top three buttons on my blouse.

"Yes?" he asked, looking surprised to be called back and eyeing my cleavage.

I walked up to him, so close I could feel his warm breath on my face. He began to look visibly nervous.

"Do you have any more deliveries?" I asked.

He shook his head and said, "No. That was it for the day."

"Good," I said, grabbing his hand and pulling him into my

office and slamming the door behind us--just in case.

"Is there something I can help you with?" he asked, wringing his hands and looking a little unsure.

"You bet," I said, placing one of my soft hands on his chest, resting my palm on his defined chest. "I know you thought you were done with work, but I think there's one delivery I really need you to make…"

My hand began to travel down his chest, over his stomach, down to his crotch area. I could feel his young, virile erection straining to burst out of his tight faded jeans. I was correct in guessing the guy was hung. I could feel his cock pulsate under the pressure of my hand.

He began to blush deeply, and I could have sworn I could see his heart beating through his chest.

"Sorry, again I didn't have much of a tip to give you, but maybe you can give me yours..." I dropped to my knees and looked up at his shocked, but pleased eyes. "Take it out," I commanded.

He looked around my office, even though the door was shut.

"What if someone walks..."

"No one will. Everyone else is gone," I said reassuringly, and then forcefully repeated, "Take it out!"

Slowly he reached down and began to unbuckle his belt. This power I felt suddenly to bark orders at a hot guy, have him follow my lead made me even more excited.

He finished unzipping his fly and went to pull his dick out through the fly in his boxers. I slapped his strong hand away. "Not yet."

He smelled of masculinity and a hard day's work. I knew his cock would probably be sweaty, sticky, especially if he was uncut, and I wanted to taste every bit of what made him a young stud.

"What do you want me to do?" he asked, sounding a little unsure.

"First, I'm going to give you the blow job of your life, and then…," I reached back for my purse again, but this time pulled out a condom. "You're going to fuck me--hard! You're going to show me how well you can use your dick. Make me moan like I'm your bitch. Understand?"

He nodded and licked his lips, his breathing getting heavier.

I could see the precum soaking through his underwear now. God, I bet this young buck would taste hot- salty, musty- manly. Ryan usually came after just a few licks, so what I considered my great cock sucking skills just went to waste while dating him. And he always acted like he had did me a favor by cumming so soon, but I enjoyed nursing on a hot, slippery manpole.

I reached in and pulled out his unbelievably hard cock. It popped out of his boxers, glad to be finally be free, and his precum dripped down my head. He was a nice seven and a half inches at least, a dark brown with a dark red head poking out of a good inch of foreskin.

"You're uncut," I say, still on my knees and looking up at him.

"That okay?" he asks. "I'm probably a little sweaty and dirty down there."

"I hope so. Don't worry. I'll clean your skin out real good for you," I replied.

I then took his foreskin in my mouth and began to tease it with my tongue. He tasted hot and salty, and there didn't seem to be an end to the precum that dripped out of his piss slit. Every time I pulled back my mouth, a long string of precum from his dick to my mouth still connected us.

"That felt so good," he moaned. "Damn, I needed that."

I pushed his back against the wall and aggressively position his cock over my mouth.

"I'm just getting started," I said. "And you better not cum until I tell you to. Understand?"

"Hell, yeah, *mami*," he muttered.

As I started to deep throat him, I thought about how good this hard mantool would feel inside me. It'd been a long time since I had a guy fuck my tight tranny pussy.

When it looked like he might cum soon I stopped and stood up-waiting for his dick to calm down some. I didn't want him to shoot his load too fast once he got up in my hole.

I ripped open the condom package with my teeth and growled, "You ready to fuck me, big guy?"

"Hell, yeah," the delivery guy said.

I looked down at his dick and saw it was twitching in anticipation of my hole.

I unzipped the back of my skirt and let it fall around my ankles, followed by panties. My seven inch hard, pink cock bobbed at attention. His eyes widened.

"That's different. Really different. I like. Fuck, let me see that she-male dick," the delivery boy said, reaching over and stroking my cock a little. "You need to get fucked bad, huh, bitch?"

I could tell he was getting over his shyness and a dominant demeanor was coming out. I liked it.

"I need a cock like yours inside me," I said.

I handed him the condom, walked over to my desk, and bent

over.   I looked back to see him putting the rubber on his dick.

"You got lube, girl?" he asked.

"Nah, just use your spit," I said, reaching back and pulling my ass cheeks apart to tempt him with my pink hole.

He spit in his hand, walked over, and rubbed his mouth juice against my hole.   I felt myself begin to shiver in anticipation.

"Do it!" I begged.

"Don't worry.   I'm going to fuck you hard, but you're goin' to like it."

I felt the tip of his dickhead pressing against my hole, demanding entrance.   I took a deep breath to relax, but before I knew it his cock worked its way into my hole with a determination and fierceness I had never felt before. Pain shot through my body, and I let out a quick cry. This only served to entice him more as he pounded harder, his balls slapping my ass cheeks with every thrust.

The pain began to turn to pleasure, and his mantool began to poke and prod my prostate.

"Oh, fuck!" I cried.

"Yeah, bitch!" he shouted at me, before collapsing on my backside and letting out a loud series of grunts.

I could feel my ass muscles tighten around his cock, and his dick spewing out its sweet nectar in the rubber.

"Damn, girl. We should fuck around some more," he said between panting breaths while still inside me.

That's when I thought that maybe I would call Ryan later after all and thank him for the perfect delivery. But I knew now, for definite, that no matter what happened, Ryan's services were no longer needed.

This
End
Up

Estimated Arrival Date: Today.

    I logged on to the Parcel Service website. I was expecting my "Anal Avenger" from Dildo-World.com. Online shopping is great! So convenient, especially since I was so busy working second shift assistant manager of a chic boutique hotel in town. I was normally home when packages came so I had gotten pretty friendly with the lesbian delivery woman, Cherie. She had a little crush on me and she'd joke about all my little naughty packages I'd get, and we'd discuss all the latest on dildo and vibrator technology. We both loved our toys.

She usually came in after twelve, so I decided to go for a quick run on the beach. I live on a bluff overlooking the Pacific. It was very motivating seeing all the local college hotties cycling, running or rollerblading on the path. It was fun fantasizing about one of them once I got home using one of my dildos. I was just coming back from the run, very sweaty and sporting my nylon shorts that wrapped around my perfect bubble butt. Another online buy. It was a hot morning, so I wore my sports bra tank top, showing off my tits and my flat tummy. I saw the familiar brown delivery truck in front of my place I couldn't help but say hi to Cherie. The steel door leading to the back was open so I yelled in.

"Hey, girl! Got a package for me?" I said as I approached the side of the truck, placing my hands around the side opening.

"Excuse me?" a deep voice echoed back. Cherie was butch, but not that butch. I could hear the boots shuffling over the steel floor and out came a stunning example of maleness. He was tall, broad-shouldered, tanned brown skin, wavy black hair, goatee and whose shorts barely contained a massive bulge above beefy thighs.

I inhaled sharply, slightly embarrassed. "Er, hi. Sorry. I thought you were Cherie," I stammered.

"Naw, she took a vacation day today. My name's Mick." Was it my imagination or was Mick eyeing my sweaty feminine body? "Did you have a good run?" he asked with a smile. Perfect teeth. Of course.

"Oh, yeah. I don't mean to bother but did you have something for me today? I live right here," I said, pointing my manicured finger to my humble landscaped abode.

"Yeah, I think so. I was looking for it a second ago..." he said as he went through the door leading to the back of the truck.

He yelled from inside, "Here it is. Something from 'D World, Inc. It got a little damaged when the sorters packed it into the truck."

Mick handed me the practically crushed box and the clearly labeled "Anal Avenger" dildo was practically slipping out. He saw my disappointed face and said consolingly, "It looks like the merchandise is still okay."

I took it out of the box. It was bigger in real life than the picture online. "Should I write a strongly worded email to corporate headquarters?" I half-joked.

He laughed back. "If it makes you feel better, I actually have the same one at home. It's a pretty tough toy. I guess we both have similar tastes," Mick said while eyeing my tits and ass and smiling that smile. "Why don't you come here in back and fill out a complaint form? Either that or we can make sure it still works. I'm actually on break right now..."

"Well, if you insist. Since I'm in the hospitality business, I'm all about excellent customer service, too," I replied climbing into the truck.

He motioned me inside and closed the door. It was a cramped space, hardly any room for his burly physique, let alone another person. A textured slip-proof steel floor and open shelves lined the inside along with a lone light above. He took the dildo package from me and set it aside on a nearby shelf.

Mick pushed me against the back of the metal door, and my

sweaty back chilled once it touched the surface. He was looking at me in his brown uniform, one hand keeping the door shut, the other hand slipped under my nylon running shorts, grabbing my ass, fingering my twitching asshole and discovering my own surprise package.

His eyes locked with mine. "Ah, this is a nice discovery," he said about my hardening cock. Around his neck a gold chain delineated a border of brown chest hair peeking above his uniform's neckline.

"I'll have to scan your package first."

I looked over to the dildo box on the shelf. "No, not that package, he said, "...this one..."

He took his barcode scanner from his rear pocket and starting rubbing it around my crotch. It was the size of brick but plastic and rounded at the edges. The red laser was displaying fun patterns against the nylon fabric which the scanner easily glided over. He grabbed my hips and turned me around so that I faced the metal door. He took the scanner and rubbed it between my ass cheeks. It was turning me on! I could feel my dick tentpoling through my shorts.

"My scanner's having trouble reading it. I'll have to do it manual inspect." He set the scanner down and easily dropped my shorts down to my ankles while he went down on his knees. He stuck his tongue into my smooth sweaty hole and reveled in its salty funk.

I moaned with pleasure. His neatly trimmed goatee felt really nice rubbing around my ass as his tongue plunged deeper into hole.

He stood up grabbed my "Anal Avenger" box and took the massive sex toy in his hand. It was about a foot long, translucent green (I always try to be eco-friendly) with raised bumps along the sides. A large head was on one end, and a handle (for better control, Dildo-Word's website explained) at the other.

"Yup, just like the one I have at home," Mick said holding it up so that the overhead light illuminated it like an emerald crystal. "It doesn't look damaged, but we'll have to try it out first."

He forced me down onto the steel ridged floor. The back of my head and neck was up against the door while he rested my legs onto the shelves on each side of the truck. My quivering asshole was vulnerable to his every whim and eagerly awaited anything he had to give.

He took off his shirt and revealed a muscular torso with hair over his chest and stomach. The overhead light silhouetted his wide body. He unzipped his shorts and I could see his massive erection through his loose cotton boxers. His dick head was peeking through a spot soaked in precum.

His work had toned every muscle on his body and the sun and give his skin a nice, healthy glow. A tattoo on one arm spelled out "USMC." Nice. Delivery guy and former Marine? I was practically creaming at the thought of it all.

He knelt down over my crotch and my exposed ass. He stuck two fingers in my mouth that I sucked hungrily, tasting the dirt under the fingernails of his big, rough hands. With one quick motion, he took his fingers out of mouth and placed them at the entrance of my asshole. The moistened fingertips slipped in easily, and I groaned with ecstasy.

He pulled out and grabbed the "Anal Avenger" and rubbed it over my dick and balls and the crevice between my ass cheeks. He licked it all over eyeing me the whole time. "Are you ready for it, baby?" he growled.

"Oh, God, Mick. Stick it in me!" I pleaded.

The huge green head was at my tight sphincter. I concentrated, anticipating the initial pain but thinking beyond it, like when holding a long pose in yoga class. Mick firmly shoved the monstrosity in my ass. Waves of pleasure emanated from my ass and crotch traveled up my spine. I inhaled sharply and almost passed out from the overwhelming feeling.

He pumped me with smooth strokes and could see I was enjoying it. My ass was tight but stretched to accommodate the huge toy.

"Now it's time for the real delivery," he said. He took the dildo out of my ass and set it inside the original box. He looked for his brown uniform and took a wrapped pre-lubed condom from his shirt pocket. He sheathed his dick and put my legs around his shoulders. I could feel his pulsing dick looking for the entrance to my tight hole. His dick head found it, and he shoved his manmeat into my hot, aching hole. It was loosened up a little after the dildo, but I wasn't prepared for the thickness of his dick. It was like shoving a beer can into me.

His fucking was confident and deliberate. Mick would pound until he got close and slowed the pace down, asking me periodically if I was alright. Sometimes he'd pull all the way out and then shove the whole girth of his dick inside me. He bent down and kissed my lips and our tongues intertwined. His goatee brushed against my smooth face. I could feel the rough textured steel floor on my back with each thrust as he laid his massive build over me. I concentrated on opening my ass to fill it with every inch of his manhood and used my ass muscles to squeeze the cum out of him. Again and again he poked and prodded my prostate, the whole time my dick oozed precum onto my stomach as I rubbed it with one hand. I massaged by breasts and savored the pleasure. Beads of sweat formed on his forehead and tip of his nose. He was working my ass into sweet agony. I had a virtuoso top playing my ass like no one has had before.

After what seemed like an eternity, he made a few more deep, slow thrusts and pulled out of me, quickly removed the condom and froze. He held his dick over me, his neck and shoulders tightening, bit his tongue with those white teeth, while his cock exploded shot after shot of manseed over my stiff dick, stomach and tits. After seeing his dick erupt, my own started to spill over onto my stomach as our fluids pooled and mixed with my sweat over by stomach.

He lay on top of me, while we both were catching our breaths, kissing me tenderly and holding me in a warm embrace.

"Thanks for the delivery," I said with a satisfied smile.

"No, thank you! That was one delivery I didn't mind making. Oh, before I forget..." He took his barcode scanner and scanned the shipping label on the nearby "Anal Avenger" box. He handed me the scanner and a stylus and said, "Please sign on the dotted line. We still have to keep to company policy."

On the touchscreen I signed my name and drew a nice, big smiley happy face. That was one delivery I definitely won't be returning...

Cable Box

I plunged my she-male cock into the young guy's tight, deep bubble ass. His ass crack had a good couple of inches before even hitting his hole which created a hot, intense slapping noise every time I went in for another long, rhythmic slide into his guy pussy.

"Oh, fuck, bitch" he cried, his face buried into one of my sofa pillows with me lying on top of his back.

"You like that? A girl like me pounding your hole? Tell me how much!" I demanded, my mouth pressed next to his ear, taking in his scent of sweat and lust. His dark spiky hair, that he had obviously spent so much time making into one of those part faux-mohawk looks, smelled of fresh soap.

"Yeah," he moaned, like a girl taking it for the first time. "It hurts, but hurts so good."

"It's because you just want to really be a bitch for someone, huh?"

"Please," he begged.

I pulled my cock out of his ass slowly, leaving only the tip of the head inside his twitching asshole.

"Say it again!" I commanded, while tossing back my long curly brown hair, this time louder, my voice even deeper.

"Please!" he whimpered.

I could see a tear sliding down the side of his cheek and onto the pillow.

"That's better!" I shouted at him, and then with as forceful and powerful of a thrust as I could muster, I slammed my cock into his ass, making him scream in part agony and part pleasure as I felt my own cock shoot jism in a volcanic semen eruption.

A couple of hours earlier I never would have imagined all of this taking place. I had been sitting at my computer trying to write an article on where t-gals could buy clothes comfortably for the local transgender mag, *Transitions Today*. I wrote at least an article a week. It sure wasn't anything glamorous, but it helped pay the bills as I worked on getting my screenwriting career off the ground in Hollywood.

Recently, I had to buy a new computer, an unwanted extra expense, but I decided to get a faster internet connection to also help me update my transgender history website. And since the cable company would hook up the internet connection, I figured I'd splurge and get a few extra channels to feed my addiction for reality shows starring anorexic females.

The trans-friendly clothing stores article was getting nowhere. I went into a few of the chain stores and since I could pass, all of them were pretty hassle free, but I knew some of my "bigger" sisters probably wouldn't be so lucky. I had a little writer's block since I'd been so swamped with work I hadn't even had time to shoot a load of girl juice in three days and four hours (yeah, I keep track).

The phone rang, and it turned out to be the cable guy arriving and wanting to come up. I told him I'd be down in a sec since the buzzer was currently broke (cheap ass landlord).

I headed down in some baggy USC shorts and a gray tank top. I expected an overweight, sweaty old guy- just like every other cable guy that I had had stop by before. But when I made it to the door, I was pleasantly surprised to find a young guy, no more than twenty, waiting for me. His pants hung a little low, a little conveniently low if you asked me. He had a bit of a crooked smile and blue eyes contrasted by dark skin. I knew I'd enjoy watching this guy put down some cable lines in my place.

"Sorry, the door buzzer is broken," I said, opening the door and letting him in.

"It's cool, ma'am," he said, walking in with his bag of tools.

We stood by the elevator and waited in a moment of awkward silence. He appeared a little nervous for some reason, and all I could think about was how I wanted to pull those baggy pants down and fuck him up his hot little butt, not before getting a taste of that sweet hole first though.

Finally, the elevator door opened, and we both walked inside, and I could have sworn I caught the guy checking out my bubble butt that showed slightly through the loose shorts.

"I wondered what took ya so long. Didn't know if I caught you in the middle of a bath or something," he said, before blushing. "Sorry, ma'am. I shouldn't have said that. Sometimes things come out before I think them over."

"No problem," I said, smiling. "The bath can wait. I have to get a little dirtier first…"

He smiled slightly before averting his eyes.

The elevator door opened, and we headed to my apartment.

Once inside, he said, "I should have all of this up and running for you in a few minutes."

"No rush," I said, sitting back on my sofa. "Do what you need to do."

He nodded, and I knew he could feel my eyes gazing up and down over his body, pausing for a second, at his nice biceps poking out of the sleeves of his work shirt. He began to look a little self-conscious, but then I could swear the young guy started showing off for me, bending down in front of me giving me a better idea of his ass.

My she-dick began to get hard in my shorts, and I started to wonder if I should have put on some underwear.

"How long you been doing this?" I asked, making it sound a little seductive.

He stood back up and turned around to face me.

"Kinda new to it," he said.

I knew we both weren't talking about the job. I could see it in his eyes.

Feeling bold, and extremely horny, I stood up, and my stiff cock created a tent in my shorts.

The guy's eyes widened, but he didn't move.

"Do you always work in delivery of your materials?" I asked, enjoying his eyes fascinated and going from my crotch to my ample bosom.

He slowly shook his head and said, "Mostly, but I've been kind of hoping to get into receiving."

"Oh, yeah," I said, walking closer to him.

"Yeah," he said, sounding a little breathless. "But it's hard to get in sometimes if you don't know someone who can take you there."

"Maybe you just haven't met the right...*co-worker*, the one who can open that do for you" I replied.

"Maybe not," he said, nodding.

I walked even closer until we could both feel each other's breaths on our faces. I imagined his heart beating rapidly under the work shirt that had his name

"Rod" embroidered on the left side.

I leaned into his ear and whispered, "Turn around, boy."

He hesitated for only a second before turning around. I wrapped my arms around his body and squeezed him tight, my cock pressing against his backside. "Like that?" I asked, while gently kissing his neck.

"Damn, girl. Fuck, yeah," he said.

I lifted his work shirt up from behind and got a glimpse of his boxers peeking out of the low rider navy blue pants. I couldn't wait anymore, and in one swift move I grabbed the sides of his pants and underwear and jerked them down going down myself with my face planted right in the crack of his ass.

"Bend over," I ordered.

The guy bent over bracing himself against my wall with his hands, and I caught the musty tempting smell of his crack. I dived my tongue straight for that hole of his, and he immediately moaned in pleasure.

"Damn," he muttered, as I began to tongue fuck him and lick the sides of the crack of his hot bubble ass.

"Like getting your ass eaten?" I groaned taking in the sweet funky smell of this young guy's hole.

"Yeah, girl," he cried. "Eat my ass!"

But I stopped and stood up. The guy, uncertain froze, and stood there with his pants and underwear down around his ankles.

"I'm going to give you what you really want now. What you know you need?"

"What's that?" he asked, his voice cracking slightly.

I reached over to a side table and pulled out a rubber and a bottle of lube.

"I'm going to fuck your ass with my she-male dick and turned you into the pussy you've always wanted to be."

I could hear him swallow hard, but he said nothing.

I unrolled the condom, and then put a generous amount of lube all over the guys pink pucker hole causing him to moan again.

"You ready, dude?" I asked.

I heard him swallow again before he said, "Yeah."

And then I plowed my cock up in his hole giving this guy what I imagined he'd been wanting for a *very* long time.

Meat Lovers

Pizza is like sex. When it's good, it's pretty good. When it's bad, it's still pretty good.
-- **Anonymous**

I was resigning myself to a boring Saturday night at home. My date ("Interior Design Guy" as my friend Brooke calls him) cancelled just a couple of hours ago.

"Work's been CRAZY. The client is demanding that new designs be emailed tonight for a conference call on Monday..." he explained.

Whatever. It's not an addition to the Louvre or anything. He's designing a new bathroom for the local Braille Institute for chrissakes. I'm sure most of the patrons won't know or care how it looks as long as the toilet paper's within arms' reach. How hard can it be?

Plus my new neighbors upstairs from me were throwing a housewarming party but they failed to tell their guests what apartment number the party was in. Since my apartment was at the front, I kept getting random people knocking on my door. That got old. Real fast.

You'll have to excuse me. I guess I'm just a little upset. It would've been date #2 with Interior Design Guy (a.k.a. Wayne), and I was looking forward to getting beyond the making out and the feeling each other up that we did after date #1. Especially after a long week at the office.

I really needed to unwind and take a long, hot shower and start my evening over again. So I took off my cute new top that nicely accentuated my tits and sloughed off my tight jeans. There was no underwear to take off since I was hoping to have Wayne's lips around my hard she-male dick sooner rather than later after dinner for dessert. I caught a glimpse of my body in the full length mirror on my closet door.

Not bad. Round bubble butt. Nice tits. Smooth skin. Long, shiny hair. All those years of yoga had turned my body into a lean, mean tranny machine.

Since I wasn't having a date tonight, I decided after the

shower I could check out the sexy pics on m4trannymeat.com and play with myself. I was gonna get off tonight come hell or high water!

I was about to get into the shower when I heard a knock on the door. I grabbed a towel and wrapped it around me. *Probably another lost soul bearing wine for that housewarming.* I opened the door as I was saying, "Oh the party is down the hall and upsta..." but the words got caught in my throat when I saw before me the dreamiest man standing on my welcome mat--holding a pizza.

"Did you order a large sausage?" he asked in a gruff voice, seemingly unfazed that I was only wearing a towel.

He was a tall, husky football

player type guy with dark hair and eyes. He had a barrel sized chest under his shirt and the name tag read "Grunt." His sensual looking mouth was encircled by a neatly trimmed goatee. The words "Three Guys from Italy" were printed in large letters on the pizza box.

"Umm, I didn't order a pizza...," I told him staring at his beautiful eyes and strong square jaw, "...but I wished I had!" I punctuated it with a wink and a smile.

The stud cracked a little grin.

"I have a feeling that pizza is for my neighbors down the hall and upstairs...er, Grunt," I continued to say, pointing him in the right direction.

He eyed me from head to toe and his gaze lingered around the towel covering by stiffening cock. "Thanks for the info, miss," he said. Before he went to make his delivery, he paused at the door and said: "If you still want that large sausage, call the restaurant in the next few minutes. I've only got one more delivery for the night. Tell 'em you want Grunt."

"You're on," I quickly replied, batting my eyelashes. He gave me the number for "Three Guys from Italy," and I quickly called on my phone. A noticeably Asian accent answered the phone. I placed my order, gave him the address and asked specifically for "Grunt" to deliver.

"Okay, no problem, lady.

Thirty minutes, okay?" the voice said on the phone.

"Yes, thank you," I said as I hung up the phone. I was brimming with excitement. I tidied up the bedroom a bit and stuck all the dirty clothes into the closet. I put all the crusty dishes into the dishwasher. I put a tank top and some shorts on, spritzed myself with a little perfume and waited patiently.

Twenty eight minutes and 37 seconds later there was a knock on my door.

I opened the door and there was Grunt not in his "Three Guys From Italy" uniform but wearing a white shirt, tie and black slacks holding a pizza.

"Did you order a large

sausage?" he said with a smile.

"Oh, yes, I did. Please come in. You sure clean up good." I ushered his beautiful body into the apartment and shut the door. I could see his perfectly sculpted butt as I locked the door.

I took the pizza from him and set it on the nearby table. I took the end of his tie and drew him close to me. His scent was an intoxicating mix of garlic, cheese, tomato sauce and that new cologne advertised by that hottie British soccer player. *Very hot.*

"How much do I owe you?" I asked.

"Nothing if you play your cards right. The pizza's free if I can make a delivery up that tight ass of yours..." he said while pawing at my butt cheeks with his thick fingers. His mouth came over mine and I succumbed to his sensual lips and probing tongue. His goatee rubbed over my face, sending waves of pleasure down my spine and into my aching crotch.

"Well, it is a tough economy right now. With high food prices, we consumers have to do what we can to get by..." I said.

Grunt ripped my tank top and shorts off and revealed my tits and engorged cock. Gobs of precum were forming at the tip and about to drop to the carpeted floor. He took one of his thick fingers and rubbed my she-semen over the head, teasing my piss slit.

"Boy, am I lucky. I love me some she-male meat. Where's the

bedroom?" he said in a calm deep voice. I pointed the direction with my eyes. He raised me over one of his broad, beefy shoulders, my ass in the air and carried confidently into the bedroom. He threw me onto the bed, as I stared at him longingly.

Grunt was in control, and he knew it. Every time I tried to reach for his dick he'd push me back on the bed.

"Hold on. We've got all night, baby," Grunt chuckled. He did a slow striptease for me as I lay on the bed. First his shoes that revealed what must have been a size 13 foot. *Lucky me.* Then he slowly undid his tie. Then his shirt buttons--first the sleeves and then the front, revealing a muscular chest covered in a forest of hair. My nipples hardened and my balls were straining at the sight of his body.

He then unbuckled his leather belt and slowly pulled it from the loops of his neatly creased slacks. I could see the bulge in his crotch forming down the side of one leg. He undid the button at the top of his pants and I could see the top of his dark, curly pubes. I was hypnotized by his every move. He painstakingly unzipped his pants in what seemed like an eternity.

"Are you ready, baby?" he asked.

I simply nodded, staring at his crotch. This man had me hooked. He dropped his pants, and

I beheld his erect manlihood. I gasped at the size and girth of it.

"Where's the protection?" he asked. I pointed to a bedside table and a drawer with all the accoutrements. He opened up the condom packaging and rolled it onto his dick. He took some lube and made sure his member was adequately covered. He took one lubed finger and stuck it up my ass to loosen up my sphincter. I moaned in anticipation.

He knelt on the bed, grabbed both my ankles as I lay on by back. His dickhead was positioned over my vulnerable ass. He stared at me, waiting. "Oh, God, Grunt. Fuck me now, PLEASE." I begged.

"I'm gonna fuck you from here

to kingdom come. But I want one thing. Under no circumstance do you touch your dick. You're gonna come when I want you to come. Understood?" he growled. It wasn't a question.

I nodded in acquiescence.

What followed was hours of ass pounding sex. Grunt took me on my back, on my stomach and lifted me up on my knees doggy style grabbing my hair. Each position his stiff dick would prod my ass until I felt I was going to burst. I fought the instinct to grab my throbbing dick as he thrust his large sausage deeper and deeper into me.

"Grunt, I don't know how much more I can take of this," I moaned. It was true. My ass had never endured such a pounding from anybody. He looked like he was enjoying the exquisite agony he was inflicting on me.

He pulled out for moment and said: "You're gonna sit on it and then I'm gonna make you come."

He laid on his back, legs spread, with his dick point straight up. I squatted over his dick and guided the tip to my aching hole. "Trust me," he said tenderly. "You're gonna love it." I could see the sincerity in his eyes, and I submitted my ass and the rest of my body to him.

He grabbed my hips, and with his massive arms, he thrust me onto his dick. He pummeled my ass and prostate. My tits jiggled with every thrust. My she-dick was dribbling precum down the shaft and was starting to puddle at the top of my balls.

"You feel so good. Your ass is so tight, girl. I wanted to fuck you as soon as you opened the door. You're so fucking hot!" he said.

"Oh, Grunt. Oh, fuck!" I yelled. His hands were firmly guiding my hips. I was leaning back, holding onto his muscular spread legs behind me for support.

"We're gonna come together, baby," he moaned while biting his tongue. He made a few more massive thrusts and then with one final push he pounded my prostate with his dickhead. That last bit forced me over the edge and my ass, prostate, balls and dick spasmed. Shot after shot of my hot seed erupted onto Grunt's stomach and chest.

"Oh, FUCK!" I yelled while my body trembled in ecstasy.

"Oh, shit, babe, I'm coming too," he hissed through gritted teeth. I could feel his massive member expanding inside my tight ass as he orgasmed.

He pulled me close to him: our hearts still beating wildly, our sweaty cocks sticking to each other and our lungs were trying to catch a breath. His semi-hard dick was still firmly up my ass. He smiled and kissed me tenderly.

"You're mine now, you know that," he whispered, massaging one of my breasts.

Yes. I didn't have to say it.

The next morning, we finished the cold pizza left out the night before. Grunt explained how "Three Guys From Italy" is actually one guy from Hong Kong. Authenticity notwithstanding, the pizza was actually pretty good. Even better is that lately I've been enjoying a regular delivery of Grunt's large sausage...

The End

About Blake Worthington

At the tender age of twenty-nine,
Blake became fascinated with all
things gender non-conformist.
Soon Blake was enthralled with all
things that made us question
gender- and sexual- identity.

Blake hopes you like Blake's
stories.

Email Blake at,
blakew@chancespress.com.